Copyright © 2019 Clavis Publishing Inc., New York

Originally published as *Een kusje voor Giraf* in Belgium and Holland by Clavis Uitgeverij,
Hasselt—Amsterdam, 2017
English translation from the Dutch by Clavis Publishing Inc., New York

Visit us on the Web at www.clavis-publishing.com.

A Kiss for Giraffe written by Judith Koppens and illustrated by Suzanne Diederen

ISBN 978-1-60537-407-9

This book was printed in January 2019 at Wai Man Book Binding (China) Ltd. Flat A, 9/F., Phase 1,
Kwun Tong Industrial Centre, 472-484 Kwun Tong Road, Kwun Tong, Kowloon, H.K.

First Edition
10 9 8 7 6 5 4 3 2 1

A **KISS** for Giraffe

Judith Koppens & Suzanne Diederen

Clavis

NEW YORK

Giraffe and Piggy are best friends.
Piggy wants to give Giraffe a kiss, but Giraffe is too tall.
"How can I reach you?" Piggy asks.

Piggy has an idea.
"I'll dig a hole for you. When you sit
in the hole, I can give you a kiss."
Piggy digs and digs.

But the hole isn't deep enough.
Piggy still can't give Giraffe a kiss.

Piggy has another idea.
"I'll swing on a rope
to give you a kiss."

He sways and swings, as high up as he can.
But he can't swing high enough.
Piggy still can't give Giraffe a kiss.

Piggy has another idea.
"I'll run toward you very fast and
then I'll jump up high to give you a kiss."

Piggy puts on his running shoes.
He runs to Giraffe as fast as he can.
Then he jumps up high.
But Piggy still can't give Giraffe a kiss.

Piggy has one more idea.
"I'll get a big ladder and
climb up to give you a kiss."

Piggy slowly climbs up the ladder.
But, oh, it's too wobbly. And then . . .

Whoops!
Piggy falls to the ground.

"Piggy!" Giraffe calls. "Are you okay?"
Giraffe bends down to give Piggy a kiss.
"Now, why didn't I think of that?" asks Piggy with a smile.
And Piggy gives Giraffe a kiss too!